What I Saw in the Teachers' Lounge

by Jerry Pallotta

SCHOLASTIC INC.
New York   Toronto   London   Auckland
Sydney   Mexico City   New Delhi   Hong Kong

Illustrated by
Howard McWilliam

I saw Ann Stearns and Nancy Howard
in the teachers' lounge.
—J.P.

For little Rufus, with love
—H.W.

ISBN 978-0-545-38472-8

Text copyright © 2012 by Jerry Pallotta
Illustrations copyright © 2012 by Howard McWilliam

12 11 10 9 8 7 6 5 4 3 2 1   12 13 14 15 16 17/0

Printed in Singapore   46

First Scholastic printing, October 2012

I saw the sign
on the door at school
every day.

Teachers'
Lounge

It wasn't fair.
Why couldn't students go in there?

Oops—the door was open.
I thought I'd take a peek.

The first time I looked, I saw my teacher.

She was surfing.

Another teacher was
in full hiking gear.

She was climbing
a rugged mountain.

I took another look. The whole staff was scuba diving.

Yikes! One teacher almost got eaten by a shark.

I looked in the corner
of the lounge.

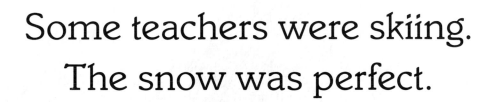

Some teachers were skiing.
The snow was perfect.

In the school cafeteria, we ate lunch.

In the teachers' lounge, they had
frog-eyeball soup, snake-brain pizza,
and elephant-toenail cupcakes.

I wondered what they tasted like.

After lunch, I peeked again.

My gym teacher was wrestling a grizzly bear.

Other teachers went for a walk in the rain forest.

They were surrounded by pretty birds.

I told my classmates everything.
They thought I was fibbing.

No one believed
a word I said. . . .

When they looked in the
teachers' lounge, nothing happened.
Everything was normal.

I peeked again.
The teachers were riding camels.

They were shopping in a market.

The kindergarten teachers
rode over to the pyramids.

I wished I could go in
the teachers' lounge.

I saw one
teacher fishing.

Other teachers were
digging for clams and
pulling lobster traps.

Don't move! Watch out!
Now the teachers were on a safari.

I saw a lion. Over there were a cheetah and some hyenas.

I watched one teacher feed a killer whale
while water-skiing.

Just then, the principal walked by.

"Get back to class," he said. "Stop peeking in the teacher.'s lounge."

I want to be a teacher when I grow up.